# KEITH

## THE CAT WITH THE MAGIC HAT

# Meet Sue and Paul:

Sue Hendra and Paul Linnet have been making books together
since 2009 when they came up with *Barry the Fish with Fingers*,
and since then they haven't stopped. If you've ever wondered
which one does the writing and which does the illustrating,
wonder no more . . . they both do both!

For Billy

## SIMON & SCHUSTER

First published in Great Britain in 2012 • This special edition published in 2021 by Simon & Schuster UK Ltd
1st Floor, 222 Gray's Inn Road, London, WC1X 8HB
Text and illustrations copyright © 2012 Sue Hendra and Paul Linnet
A CIP catalogue record for this book is available from the British Library upon request
978-1-4711-4415-8 • Printed in China • 10 9 8 7 6 5 4 3 2 1

# KEITH
## THE CAT WITH THE MAGIC HAT

by Sue Hendra
and Paul Linnet

**SIMON & SCHUSTER**
London   New York   Sydney   Toronto   New Delhi

Keith the cat was merrily minding
his own business when . . .

Wheee!

"Ha-ha-ha, Keith's got an ice cream stuck on his head!" chuckled the other cats.

Suddenly, Keith felt a little bit shy and a little bit silly.

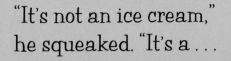

"It's not an ice cream," he squeaked. "It's a . . .

It's a...

It's a...

It's a...

This made the cats laugh even louder.
"Go on then, show us some magic!" they chortled.

Poor Keith! What was he going to do?
"W-w-well, first," he stammered,
 "I need my magic wand."

He reached for the chocolatey magic
wand on the ground but . . .

It started to run away –
ALL by itself!

The cats were amazed.
"Wow, Keith! You made
it move," they gasped.

Keith was amazed too . . . but he didn't say anything.
"More!" the cats cried, excitedly.
"More magic. More! More!"

Keith took a deep breath.
Then he waved his wand around . . .

"Abracadabra!"

But nothing happened.

Keith tried again.

"Alacazoo!"

Still nothing happened.

The cats were getting impatient.
They chanted and stamped their feet.
"MORE! MORE! MORE!"

"Whizzy-whoo-do-da!"
cried Keith, AND . . .

. . . just then, a whole family of rabbits popped out
of the ground. They'd never heard such a noise!

"Keith – you did it!" the other cats cheered.
"You magicked up some rabbits. Hooray!"

They were all having such a fun time
that they didn't hear a distant WOOF!

WOOF! WOOF! WOOF!

"Yikes! A dog! Quick, Keith, save us with your magic!" the cats squealed in panic.

# WOOF! WOOF! WOOF!

But, of course, Keith couldn't REALLY do magic.
What was he going to do?

The cats ran up the tree.

They looked down at the barking dog. "Quick, Keith, DO something!" they cried.

Then . . .

Whoops!

Keith's magic hat slipped off his head.
It was falling quickly through the air . . .

"Oh no! Your magic hat!" cried the cats.
"Now you'll NEVER be able to make
the dog disappear."

Keith felt terrible.
"It's not a magic hat," he admitted sadly.
"You were right all along – it's just an ice cream,
and now we are stuck up this tree FOREVER!
I'm sorry!"

But then . . .

"Hooray for Keith!" cried the cats.
"You're magic even without your hat!"
"Thank you," said Keith shyly. "And, for my
next trick, I will make this blob of ice cream
on the end of my nose disappear."

The cats waited patiently.

Then . . .

Keith stuck out his tongue and **licked it off!**

If you like

# KEITH
## THE CAT WITH THE MAGIC HAT

you'll love these other adventures from

# Sue Hendra and Paul Linnet